CUMBRIA LIBRARIES

D1424802

CAP'N BUCK
MONSTROUS
BIOGRAPHIES

SUNBIRD
PENGUIN

Published by Ladybird Books Ltd 2012
A Penguin Company
Penguin Books Ltd, 80 Strand, London, WC2R 0RL, UK
Penguin Group (USA) Inc., 375 Hudson Street, New York 10014, USA
Penguin Books Australia Ltd, Camberwell Road, Camberwell,
Victoria 3124, Australia (A division of Pearson Australia Group Pty Ltd)
Penguin Group (NZ), 67 Apollo Drive, Rosedale, Auckland 0632,
New Zealand (a division of Pearson New Zealand Ltd)
Canada, India, South Africa

Sunbird is a trade mark of Ladybird Books Ltd

© Mind Candy Ltd. Moshi Monsters is a trademark
of Mind Candy Ltd. All rights reserved.

Written by Lauren Holowaty

All rights reserved.
No part of this publication may be reproduced,
stored in a retrieval system, or transmitted in any form
or by any means, electronic, mechanical, photocopying,
recording or otherwise, without the prior consent
of the copyright owner.

www.ladybird.com

ISBN: 978-1-40939 - 060-2
001 - 10 9 8 7 6 5 4 3 2 1
Printed in China

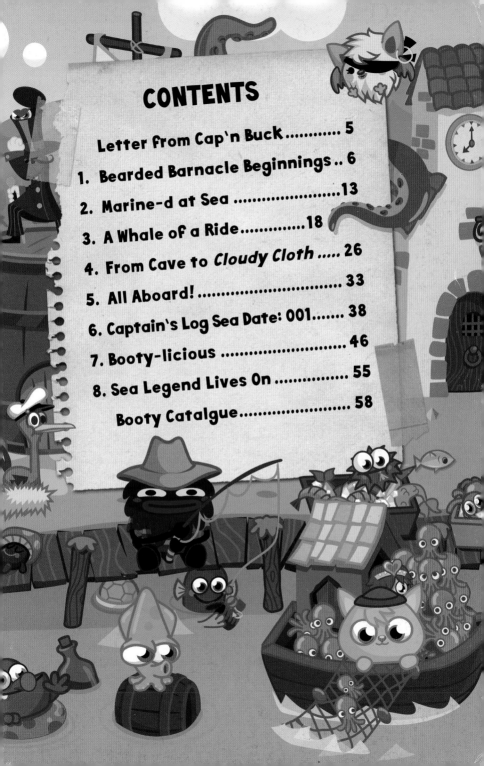

CONTENTS

ARRR!

AHOY THERE, ME HEARTIES! WELCOME TO THIS BOOTY-FUL BOOK ABOUT ME OL' LIFE AND TIMES. I BET YOUSE CANNA WAIT TO READ IT. I DID TRY TO WRITE A BOOK FOR YE MESELF, BUT THIS BE ABOUT AS FAR AS I DID GET BEFORE I HADDA HEAD OFF ON ANOTHER ADVENTURE:

MY NAME IS CAP'N BUCK E. BARNACLE AND I LIKE LISTENING TO HAIROSNIFF. I BE A PIRATE AND I SAIL A BOAT CALLED THE *CLOUDY CLOTH CLIPPER*, BRINGIN' LOTS OF BOOTY T' MONSTRO CITY.

Y'SEE IT BE MUCH BETTER THAT I HAVE RUBY SCRIBBLEZ WRITING THIS HERE BOOK FOR ME. I MAY BE THE BEST PIRATE MONSTRO CITY HAS EVER SEEN, BUT I BE NOT TOO GOOD AT THIS HERE WRITIN' MALARKY.

YARRRRR!   -BUCK ⚓

Chapter 1
Bearded Barnacle Beginnings

Baby Buck's 1st Birthday!

Introduction

People often ask where the mysterious Cap'n Buck came from. So one day, I, Ruby Scribblez, was asked to go researching, delve deep into the ocean of Buck's past, and put all of the famous pirate's journals, letters and stories together, to come up with . . . well, this book really.

In this first ever published account of Buck's cockle-warming adventures, there may be one or two tall ship tales and vague imaginings, just a few puzzles yet unsolved, and quite a bit of exaggeration for emphasis, but this, dear readers, really is (quite probably) the closest to the truth you are ever likely to find. So read on and find out all you can about Monstro City's very own pioneering pirate, the one and only . . . Captain Buck E. Barnacle!

A Pirate be Born

Many moon-sters ago, right in the heart of Potion Ocean's shady shallow waters, little Buck Barnacle was born. No one seems entirely sure of the exact date, but it was probably some time around Talk Like a Pirate Day, and it was definitely before the Pussycat Poppets were born.

The son of his pa, Barry Barnacle, and his ma, Bernie Barnacle, Buck was a descendant of the crusty old Curl-footed Bearded Barnacle family.

The Curl-footed
Bearded Barnacle Family

But Buck was no ordinary Barnacle. He was by far the hairiest bearded barnacle any seafaring creature ever did see. In fact, he was one of the hairiest creatures ever to have been seen in the sea! Not one of his enormous family (it is rumoured that he had around five thousand brothers and three thousand sisters), had as much hair on their beards as little Buck had on his fluffy little elbows.

"Hairy-Bucky, Hairy-Bucky, Hairy-Bucky!" Buck's brothers and sisters would tease, over and over again.

"Arrrrr!" Buck would reply, as he hadn't learnt any other words yet.

It didn't take long for the nickname 'Hairy-Bucky' to stick to Buck, and not one of the 8002* other Bearded Barnacles, ever used his real name again.

While we're on the subject of things sticking, it is probably important to mention here that Bucky, Barry, Bernie and their enormous family, were literally stuck to each other, like super glooper glue. The entire Barnacle family lived on a rock protruding out of the water and had no way of letting go of that rock, and no way of letting go of each other – they were super glooper stuck. This sticky way of life was very typical of a barnacle, and it made Bucky and his family very close and extremely clingy.

Unable to move anywhere or explore anything, all the Barnacles were, quite obviously, attached to one another. They amused themselves time and time again, by telling waves of sea jokes, as the Potion Ocean tide came in, and then repeating the jokes, as the tide went out. Tide in, tide out. Tide in, tide out. And so on.

*Estimated figure only, as no one really ever counted how many Curl-footed Bearded Barnacles there were back then. Mainly because no one cared all that much.

And Bernie and her enormous family would laugh along with Barry, wholeheartedly, as if they had never heard the joke before.

And the whole Bearded Barnacle clan would erupt in fits of hermit crab hysteria. Even though they had spent their days and nights hearing the same tropical fishy punchline, ever since they were Barnacle babies.

I don't want to bore you with any more of the blistering Barnacles' sea joke shenanigans, (you probably don't have the memory of a gold fish), so I shall simply say;

And so the waves of jokes would go on. Tide in . . . Tide out.

But the Barnacles did have one other 'porpoise' in life; distantly related to the infamous Crab Twins, and the Mobster-lobsters, (led by the Cod Father), you may not be surprised to learn that the Barnacles enjoyed a treacherous life of grime and grabbing. With no other possessions but each other, the Barnacles fought as hard as they could to grab onto anything that floated their way and claim it as their own. This included old bottles of Toad Soda, half eaten Crab and Jelly Sandwiches, and sometimes even odd bits of Furi facial hair, just for fun and furry giggles!

With the knowledge of nothing other than clinging and scavenging, and a few not-really-all-that-funny sea jokes, the life of a Barnacle was not-so-pretty and a pretty dismal one at that.

As little Bucky got bigger, he realized just how different he was from the rest of his family. Not only was he hairier, he was also beginning to realize that he hated the fact that his town had so many problems with grime. ('Grime Waves' as the Monstro City police would call them.) Bucky also had absolutely no desire to keep stealing half-used and unwanted things from the sea.

"What's the use in taking other people's stuff? I want to give everything back to its rightful owner," Bucky would say honorably. Later adding, "And go shopping for new stuff of my own!"

It soon became obvious that Bucky needed some direction in his life, and that the back and forth of the Potion Ocean tide wasn't getting him anywhere, fast.

To pass the tides and dream of a brighter and fishier future, Bucky wrote a letter to his all-time ultimate sea idol, Billy the Squid, and shoved it in an old bottle of Toad Soda, hoping that one day it just might reach him.

To claim your exclusive virtual gift, go to the sign-in page of
MOSHIMONSTERS.COM
And enter the first word on the first line of the twenty-seventh page of this book! Your surprise free gift will appear in your treasure chest!

DEAR BILLY THE SQUID*,

I HAVE ADMIRED YOU FROM ACROSS THE SEAS FOR QUITE SOME TIME. I AM LONGING FOR A NEW LIFE. HERE IS AN A-Z OF THE THINGS I DREAM OF, IN NO PARTICULAR ORDER. LET ME KNOW IF YOU CAN HELP.

- ADVENTURES ON THE OPEN WAVES. (NOTE: NOT IN THE SHADY SHALLOWS)
- BOAT TO SAIL AWAY FROM HERE
- CREW NEEDED FOR BOAT ABOVE
- DRY CLOTHES. I HAVE BEEN IN SOGGY CLOTHES FOR THE WHOLE OF MY LIFE

- EYE PATCH (JUST COZ IT'S COOL)
- FRIENDS OF THE NON BARNACLE VARIETY
- GOLD TO BUY ALL THIS STUFF
- HAT (THE ADVENTUROUS TYPE)
- INK (MY ONE SQUID INK PEN IS DRIPPING DRY AS YOU CAN SEE)
- JOKES (NEW ONES THAT AREN'T ABOUT THE SEA)
- KARATE LESSONS
- LAND, SO I CAN GET OFF MY HAIRY BOTTOM AND WALK FOR A CHANGE
- MOUSTACHE (FAKE FOR SPECIAL OCCASIONS)
- NUN CHUCKS TO HELP WITH KARATE ABOVE
- ON-BOARD PET FOR BOAT ABOVE
- PORT TO PARK MY BOAT IN
- QUENUT BUTTER SANDWICH (FRESH, FULL AND DRY, NOT HALF EATEN AND FISHED OUT OF THE SEA)
- RUBBER DUCK - FOR COMPANY IN THE BATH
- SAIL (FOR BOAT ABOVE). SWORD TO PRETEND FIGHT WITH AND SEA MONSTER MUNCH

* Note how at this point in Bucky's young life, he still wrote and spoke like a Barnacle, rather than the swashbuckling pirate we know now!

P.T.O

- TENTACLE TORCH - FOR NIGHT-TIME ADVENTURES
- UNLIMITED ULTIMATE TREASURE
- VALENTINE'S DAY CARD - I HAVEN'T EVER HAD ONE
- WORM EARRING - JUST THE ONE FOR THAT PIRATE-ADVENTURER LOOK
- (E)XERCISE - I HAVE BEEN STUCK STILL FOREVER
- YUMMY FRESH FOOD AND NOT SOGGY UNWANTED LEFTOVERS SLUNG INTO THE SEA
- Z - ZZZZ! (SOME SLEEP AFTER ALL OF THE ABOVE)

I HOPE THAT ONE DAY WE MAY MEET AND GO ON AN ADVENTURE TOGETHER!

YOURS TRULY,

BUCK BARNACLE

(PLEASE DON'T CALL ME HAIRY BUCKY.)

Reply from Billy the Squid - Found many years later. Note: Messages in bottles can sometimes be like sending something by Sea Snail Mail.

Deer Hairy Bucky,

Fank youse four writing to me.
I be criminal, so canna really read nor right.

Hope two meat u soon.

Bill e the s£

x

After this disappointing response, Buck realized he had no choice but to carry on his Bearded Barnacle days. Until one day . . .
. . . there was a terrible storm.

Chapter 2
Marine-d at Sea

It was the worst storm Monstro City and its surrounding islands had ever recorded, since records had begun, earlier that day. Evil forks of lightning spiked and pierced the clouds, and huge bucket-loads of rain came pouring down onto the sea. The wind howled through the water and the waves of Potion Ocean thrashed and crashed down on the shores. Very soon, the Bearded Barnacles' shady, shallow home was flooded with light, deep water. Their time and tide was up!

Bucky and his family clung on to each other and their rock with all their might. They tried to tell one another their usual waves of sea jokes, but this time, there was no giggling, no eruptions of laughter, and not even a hint of hermit crab hysteria. This time, each and every member of the Barnacle family was too scared to be smiling.

Every member that was, except for Bucky. As his family cried sad tears of "By barnacles, I'm scared," Bucky cried happy tears of, "By barnacles, I'm free! Free as a sea gull!"

The pull of the waves became so strong that even the super-glooper sticky glue that held Bucky close to his family became somewhat un-sticky. Soon, Bucky was literally broken free of his family ties and tentacles, by the sheer force of the water.

No one knows what happened to the 8002* other Curl-footed Bearded Barnacles, but we do know that Bucky floated and floated, far, far and away from all of them.

*As before.

He drifted away from the shady shallows and out into the open water of the sea. But Bucky still didn't cry out for help. He was excited. Finally his time for adventure had arrived!

"Whoopee!" Bucky gasped, as he bodysurfed the deep waters, ducking and diving along the way. "Like, totally rad, dude!"

Somehow Bucky managed to find some pretty awesome surf wear that was washed his way in the storm, and an outta-this-world newly waxed surfboard.

He even found time to hang ten and carve-up the waves with some new surfer buddies.

Pretty soon, Bucky and his fellow laidback sea lubbers all wiped-out, as the storm was, "Like, totally too intense, dude". They all went their separate waves, vowing to meet up again one day, if that was where the ocean took them.

The storm eased off, and Bucky came to a sudden stop right in the middle of the ocean. He floated on the surface of the water, imagining the life at sea he might now have. He was far away from the tentacle ties of the rest of his family, and with exciting new friends and scary new anemones – the world was most definitely his oyster.

"What should I do next?" Bucky asked himself as he began to nod off and dream about all the exciting adventures he could now go on . . .

Years later, we found Bucky's dream diary . . .

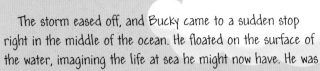

Buck's Dream Diary

During my days floating out to sea, I had three very different dreams:

Dream 1

I found myself washed up on a deserted dessert island. It wasn't a desert island, with sandy shores, but an island made entirely of dessert with candy shores. Everything looked good enough to eat, so that's what I did!

With help from a team of Psycho Gingerboys, I built a Cake House for shelter from the rain of lumpy banana custard drops. The floor was made of delicious waffles and the walls were decorated with Cotton Candy Wallpaper.

By day, I swam in pools of jellybeans, chomping on Sludge Fudge, and found a pick and mix assortment of friends. By night, I chilled on my Toffee Crunch Couch, then drifted off into sweet dreams on my bed of fluffy Marshmallow Pillows.

Dream 2

One morning, I woke up and I was a squillionaire! My Cake House had turned into a Palace. I was wearing a Prom Tuxedo, Fake Tash and Monsieur's Monacle, and I reeked of exquisite Eau de Toilet. My walls were covered floor-to-ceiling in expensive art, including the real Monsta Lisa Painting, and I had more valuables than that famous shop in Monstro City, Horrods, would be able to sell in a squillion years. There were piles of Rox everywhere – I was rich, and it felt marvellous!

I spent my days shopping with celebrity Moshis, and my nights dining on lashings and lashings of Grande Gateaux, followed by sixty-two carrot medallions of Roast Beast. It was simply divine!

Dream 3

This dream felt so real, it scared the sea-life out of me. I was sailing the Seventy Seas in a magnificent sailing ship. I was the captain, I had a shipmate named Lefty, and a big crew of monsters helping me. We toured the world looking for treasure, fought battles and braved treacherous storms. It was scary, but at the same time, it was lots and lots of fun.

We travelled as far as Bubblebath Bay. It was a wonderfully pioneering journey. Yarr! And I made an excellent pirate, even if I do say so meself.

After his amazing dreams, Bucky woke up and realized he wasn't swinging on his sweet-filled porch, or spending squillions, or even sailing across the Seventy Seas in a ship. He was in way over his head, (the sea was in fact whooshing over his head) he was alone, and he was totally out of his depth, stranded in the middle of Potion Ocean. Not only that, but Bucky had also been drifting further and further into dangerous waters. He was a castaway, lost at sea and miles away from everywhere.

Reaching out, and holding onto a hole in a strange slimy rock for dear life, Buck began to feel quite scared and home seasick. He waited and waited for something to cling on to . . . some hope or some . . .

. . . conveniently placed whale!

WHOOSHHH!

"Arrrrr!" yelled Bucky, as he was flung up into the air in an enormous spray of water. He hadn't grabbed onto a hole in a rock at all, but the waterspout of an enormous purple stripy whale, named Gail. She saw Bucky fly high in the splurting spray of water and caught him in her giant mouth.

Bucky was safe! Well, as safe as you could be inside a whale's mouth. It was pitch black, very squishy and very fishy smelling in there. It smelt like a cross between a Fishy Fountain, a mouldy Crab and Jelly Sandwich and a Cuddly Fisherman – gross!

Bucky tried to hold his breath for as long as he could. But it was no use. He could only hold it for a few seconds, and he had to breathe in heavier at the end anyway. The stench made him want to be sick. He had to try to find a way out. Life stunk if it was going to be like this.

Creeping around in the dark, Bucky felt his way along the damp, rough walls of Gail's mouth, until he came across something jingly, jangly and hanging down from the roof. He grabbed onto whatever it was and pulled hard, twice.

"HURRRP! HURRRRP" went Gail, like only a whale, or a giant cruise ship could. Then she yawned the biggest yawn in the world (this must be true because whales are the biggest creatures in the world) and Bucky dived out of her open mouth, clung onto the side of her head and climbed onto her back, just like Indiana Bones.

"Many apologies for that, my chap," gasped Gail. "I was trying to help you, not gobble you up."

"No problem," replied Bucky, a little taken aback that he could understand Whale-sh.

"So, where can I take you?" asked Gail. "Where's home?"

"I'm not sure, yet," replied Bucky. "What I'm really looking for is an adventure."

"Well, I can take you on a little tour of all the islands around Monstro City, Cap'n," said Gail. "Then, maybe you can decide where you'd like to stay."

Bucky liked being called captain and jumped at the chance to go on his first proper adventure at sea.

MONSTRO SEAS

"HURP! HURP!" went Gail, and she set off, carrying Bucky, and leading a great big giggly school of Batty Bubblefish behind her, laughing all the way.

Captain Bucky, Gail and the Batty Bubblefish began their journey by heading off towards the sweet waters of Candy Shoals. When they arrived, the friends were completely surrounded by Candy Cane Corals, and delicious delights.

"I've been here before!" gasped Bucky, then he sighed, "but only in my dreams."

"Well, now you've been here for real," said Gail, "And I'm sure you'll be back again before you know it."

After gobbling up lots of treats and stocking up on enough Jelly Beans to last them around twenty years' worth of Jelly Bean Days, they decided it was time to head off to pastures new.

Stopping off for a quick head-bang, crowd surf and jam session at Rockstar Reef, the friends glided along to Tiki Tropic to catch a bit of sun.

As soon as they got tired of Tiki's lazy days and sunrays, Gail suggested they step up the adventure a little, and zoom off to a fabulous new place she had heard waves of rumours about – Futuristic Falls.

So the gang did just that. I'm afraid I can't tell you what they saw and what they got up to there though, because you'll just have to wait for the future to see.

Back from the mysterious future to the present, Bucky and his gang gallivanted off to The Gulf of New Gizmo, where an electrifying time was had by all . . .

Feeling a little peckish after all of their travelling, the Batty Bubblefish led Gail and Bucky on to Cookhouse Quay, where they ate and ate and ate, like they'd never eaten before.

After food, it was time for a big treat at Humongous Haven. They had it large there, very large in fact, as everything on the entire island was giant! Even Gail Whale felt small.

Scaring themselves a little silly on Halloween Island, which was the most terrifying place they'd been to yet, Gail, Bucky and the school made a swift recovery, relaxing in the warm and peaceful waters of Bubblebath Bay. The Batty Bubblefish felt particularly at home, as you can imagine.

Whilst relaxing in bubble baths of loveliness, Gail asked Bucky where he would like to go for his final destination of the trip.

"I haven't actually ever set foot in Monstro City," said Bucky.

"Very well," replied Gail from her giant bubble bath, "I'll take you there first thing tomorrow morning. I should have time to wash all these bubbles off by then!"

So early the next morning, Gail took Bucky to his final port of call – Monstro City. (The Bubblefish stayed behind at Bubblebath Bay to blow bubbles for a little while longer – they just couldn't get enough!)

Monstro City is the biggest, busiest and most exciting monstrosity you have ever seen. With aqua blue mountains, lumpy bumpy hills, colourful rainbows, a giant funfair, shop-filled streets and monsters of different shapes and sizes chatting and playing, it even had its very own name in lights!

But Bucky was so tired from his fast-paced whirlwind taster of the travelling and adventuring sea-life, he didn't actually see any of Monstro City's delights or even the street lights. He was fast asleep on Gail's back, snoring away, and didn't even notice they'd arrived.

Buck slipped and slid off Gail's back without her noticing. It would have been just like an enormously fun water slide for Bucky, had he woken up to notice. But he didn't even bat a furry eyelid and continued to snooze. He flew off of her back and landed in a secret hidden cave in the shores of Monstro City. And still he slept.

(We're not sure of the cave's exact location, but we think it was probably over the volcano and faraway, so you should check it out one day, if you get the chance.)

Unaware, Gail finished her tour of the shore and swam off into the ocean, never to be seen again, or not for a few chapters of this book, at least.

(Little did she know then, that she would see Bucky back sailing the high seas again one day.)

Bucky was so exhausted from all his adventures, he slept inside the secret cave for a very, very long time. Until one day, he woke up . . .

Chapter 4
From Cave to
Cloudy Cloth

"Yarrr!" cried Bucky, as he woke up inside the hidden cave. He had no idea where he was or how he'd arrived there. He felt alone, stranded and totally seashell-shocked.

Slowly, Bucky began to recall floating away from his home, surfing, dreaming and meeting Gail and the Batty Bubblefish, and little snapshots of their travels together. He remembered visiting islands far and wide and exploring the seas. But where were Gail and the Bubblefish now? Had it all been one giant ocean of a dream? Had he simply drifted from the shady shallows to the secret cave, and dreamt up one adventure after another? Suddenly, a weird noise startled him and he forgot his boat of thought.

"Sqwark! Squelch! Sqwark! Squelch!"

Bucky peered out of the cave to investigate. He spotted a fleshy blue-green monster, with tentacles for arms and one big eye in the middle of his forehead, fumbling around on the rocks outside the cave and looking a little lost.

"Who be you?" asked the strange creature.

"Bucky," replied Bucky. "I be Bucky."

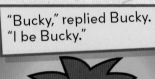

"Buck. E, what?" asked the creature.

"Barnacle," replied Buck E, thinking that Buck. E sounded much better than Bucky, and liking his newfound friend instantly.
"I see," said the creature.
"I can see," agreed Buck. E, looking into the creature's enormous eye, "and who be you?"

"Me name's Lefty," said Lefty.
"Pleasure to meet you, Lefty," said Buck E, thinking his name sounded very familiar, but he couldn't recall why.

And with that, Buck was never called Bucky again.

Buck and Lefty soon realized they both had a great deal in common. They were both from the sea and they both liked adventure. They also both found it very hard to live on land, with their shaky sea legs.

Buck was convinced he had met Lefty before at some point, as he seemed so familiar, but he still couldn't put his furry finger on why.

As a nice gesture, so they could be sea flood brothers and friends forever, Buck made a pact that he would always stand by Lefty. To show his devotion he put a patch on his left eye, so he could be the right eye, and Lefty, quite obviously could be the left eye.

One day, Buck and Lefty headed off across Monstro City in search of something, but they weren't really sure what.

They spent their days on land exploring the shores of Monstro City and meeting its monstrous inhabitants. They spent their nights dancing away at the Underground Disco to the latest Moshi smash hits. They shopped 'til they literally dropped onto the floor of the Market Place. They planted seeds to attract even the rarest of Moshlings. They served delicious Ice Scream at the Ice-Scream Shop to earn Rox to pay for all their shopping sprees, (although it has to be said that they spent most of their time actually eating the Ice Screams themselves and making the craziest topping towers out of the sprinkles.) And finally, they climbed to the very top of Mount Sillimanjaro at sunrise.

But even after all that, the duo of unlikely monsters sat at the top of the mountain, looking out to the sea, feeling that there was something missing, and it wasn't just Lefty's other eye!

What was missing they realized after a while, was stuff. Main Street and Sludge Street were full of shops, but there should be more. Surely if Buck and Lefty could get their hands on some booty, they'd do a roaring trade in Monstro City?

While they were hatching their plan to find some stuff, the friends realized that more than anything they both longed to be back on the sea again. Buck wanted to find Gail Whale and the Batty Bubblefish to say thank you, and pay them back for saving his life. Lefty wanted to discover new places and wet his tentacles for a bit.

Buck thought back to the letter he wrote to Billy the Squid when he had been knee high to a crab claw. He'd always wanted adventures on the high seas, a boat, a crew and most of all – unlimited treasure . . . There was only one thing for it – to head out into the depths of Potion Ocean and become pirates!

Buck remembered how much he liked to be called captain, so he decided to rename himself Captain Buck. E Barnacle. (Cap'n Buck to old acquaintances and friends.) It had a nice piratey ring to it. He then bought himself the essential skull and crossbones hat. Fashion guru, Tyra Fangs, had said that only pirates could get away with that sort of fashion statement, but he was a pirate, so he was sure he could work it. The flood brothers black eye patch he already wore topped off his whole 'Ooh, arrrr!' ensemble and he was dressed and ready to go.

Now, came the difficult part – learning the lingo. He knew that 'yarrr!' would work at sea, but Buck really felt he needed his own language. It had to be one that everyone could almost understand, but still allowed him to dare to be mysterious. So he tracked down a pirate speaktionary, with influences from ancient pirate lingo and set to work . . .

Pirate Speaktionary

(Especially for Cap'n Buck E. Barnacle and crew, but also useful for translation and Talk Like a Pirate Day.)

AHOY! - hello

ALOFT - upstairs

AN' - and

AVAST - stop

AYE - yes

AYE, AYE - of course, I will get to it

BE - am, are or is

BOOTY - riches that may have been stolen

CANNA - can't

CUTLASS - sword

DIDNA - didn't

DRINK, THE - Potion Ocean

FER - for

GRUB - food

HANDS - crew

JABBER - talk

JOLLY ROGER - pirate flag

LAD - young monster boy

LASS - lady monster

ME - my

NOGGIN - head

PIECES OF EIGHT (also known as booty, see above) - money/Rox

PORT - left

OFFE - off

OL' - old

OU' - out

STARBOARD - right

THAR - there

TH' - the

YE - you

YERSELF - yourself

YOUSE - you are

PIRATE LINGO

ARRRR - add to every sentence you say for pirate emphasis

SHIVER ME TIMBERS - say whenever surprised and shout it as loud as you can.

EVERYTHIN' SHIPSHAPE - make sure everything is tidy and in order

YO, HO, HO - this is how you should laugh

DASH MY BUTTONS - have a laugh

ALL HANDS ON DECK - all monsters should be on the ship's deck

LAND HO - land in sight

LAND LUBBERS - monsters who stay on land

SEA DOG - a monster pirate who has been at sea for some time

WALK THE PLANK - just do as it says!

After swotting up on the lingo, Buck and Lefty formed a seaworthy crew made up of a group of waifs and strays from in and around Monstro City. They would later be referred to as Buck's shipmates. Together they headed to The Port and built the now infamous *Cloudy Cloth Clipper*. It had an amazing poop deck, a big red main mast, a mizzen, a rudder, a captain's cabin and lots of other fancy sailing boaty things.

Very soon the *Cloudy Cloth Clipper* and its completely inexperienced captain and crew were ready to set sail for an adventure of a lifetime . . .

Do ye think we be need'n some sort of steering wheel fer this, Buck...?

Chapter 5
All Aboard!

Well, almost ready that was!

And so, after the ever so slightly important wheel and a few other sea-ssentials, including a sail and an anchor, were hastily added, the *Cloudy Cloth* was finally ready for her maiden voyage.

Buck, Lefty and the crew invited everyone they knew in Monstro City to send them off in style. Moshis and Moshlings old, young, hairy and slimy, gathered at The Port to catch their first glimpse of the vessel. Excitement was in the air. Even Roary from *The Daily Growl* had come along to report on the historical event.

A Moshi medley of sea songs was played, including 'Pirate Face', 'Bootiiful Girl' and 'Sea Super-stylin'. Every Moshi danced the sailor's jig together. (The jig looked a lot like the 'Hey Moshi' dance you and I know today, only a little wetter.)

Wearing two fake pirate eye patches (one on an eye on his face, the other on an eye on his hairdon't), a young Simon Growl was the chosen celebrity host for the send off.

"I was not surprised to have been chosen to host this event," Simon began. "After all, I am Monstro City's most senseasional sea-lebrity!"

Despite Simon's terrible attempts at joking, he didn't smile once and growled on about himself, until the crowd told him to, "Get on with it!"

"Okay, okay," howled Simon. "I name thee, Monstro City's number one top of the pirate sea charts . . . the *Cloudy Cloth Clipper*! And today shall be your first voyage. Blah de, blah de, blah."

And with that, Simon cut the Poppet Pink Ribbon tied to the ship, unveiled the hull (well, pulled the rags off of it) to reveal it in all its splendour, and smashed a bottle of Vintage Toad Soda against the side, totally showbiz style. (The bottle made a rather large hole that needed to be fixed and Simon had actually cut the ship's rigging rather than the ribbon, but it was nice and dramatic and fitting for the send off, so Cap'n Buck didn't mind too much. He asked the crew to do some last minute fixing attempts to make everything totally ship-shape.)

Cries of "Ship ahoy!", "For sea's a jolly good fellow-ship!" and the occasional, "Oh, I do like to be beside the seaside," were heard from miles around. Everyone threw confetti-like showers of Sea Monster Munch up into the air, just like Monstro City's Carnivor'all time, but without the meat.

Finally, after one last cheer, Buck and his crew were ready to take one small step onto the boat, but one enormous leap for Monstro City into the Seventy Seas.

Hoisting the flag, pulling up the anchor, and holding his Pirate Speaktionary tight, Captain Buck. E Barnacle stood proudly on deck and shouted as loudly as he could, **"I be Cap'n Buck E. Barnacle and this be my ship! Shiver me timbers, me hearties, we're off! So long ye land lubbers, arrrr!"**

From that day forward he would speak only in the language of a pirate.

As the *Cloudy Cloth Clipper* drifted out of The Port, around Gift Island, and set sail out on the high seas, the crowds waved goodbye, not knowing when they might see their Cap'n again. Little did they know it wouldn't be for quite some time, or quite what adventures would be in store for Monstro City's first and only pioneering pirate. But all they really could think of at the time was the giant shopping list of booty they had given Buck to collect on his adventures, and when they might get their stuff!

It is rumoured that on this day the infamous phrase 'With a yo, ho, ho and his Moshi crew, Buck E. Barnacle sailed the ocean blue!' came about.

To amuse themselves whilst sailing the waves, Buck, Lefty and their shipmates told pirate joke after joke. Yo, ho, ho! All the joke telling reminded Buck of his ma and pa, Bernie and Barry Barnacle. 'I be glad I'm not still stuck on a rock,' Buck thought to himself, 'but I hope ma and pa are doing okay. Maybe if I keeps travelling the high seas I will find 'em one of these days.'

And by night, they sung sea-song, after sea-song . . .

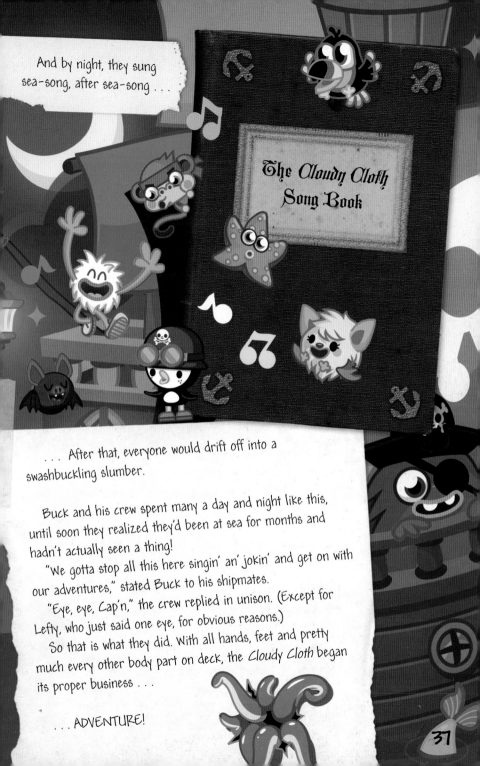

The Cloudy Cloth Song Book

. . . After that, everyone would drift off into a swashbuckling slumber.

Buck and his crew spent many a day and night like this, until soon they realized they'd been at sea for months and hadn't actually seen a thing!

"We gotta stop all this here singin' an' jokin' and get on with our adventures," stated Buck to his shipmates.

"Eye, eye, Cap'n," the crew replied in unison. (Except for Lefty, who just said one eye, for obvious reasons.)

So that is what they did. With all hands, feet and pretty much every other body part on deck, the Cloudy Cloth began its proper business . . .

. . . ADVENTURE!

Chapter 6

Captain's Log
Sea Date: 001

Day 103
Totally tropical-tastic! This here afternoon we did pick up the ol' pace a few tangled Knots or two, and made it to Tiki Tropic in Knot much time at all. That was after a tropical storm almost turned the *Cloudy Cloth* nearly upside down though, bless her little wooden deck! I canna remember th' waters being that crazy when I came here with Gail Whale all that time ago. When I think back to then I remember my dream of sailing the seas with a crew and I realize - my childhood Barnacle dreams are coming true!

Still, it be scorchin' hot here and there be plenty of smoking hot booty to take home too; Hot Hammocks, Tiki Torches, and the trees are full of Sunshine Berries - the brightest fruit around. Although not quite as bright as the glow from my red-hot sunburn! Luckily, I brought plenty of Growloe Vera Gel with me for me fur . . .

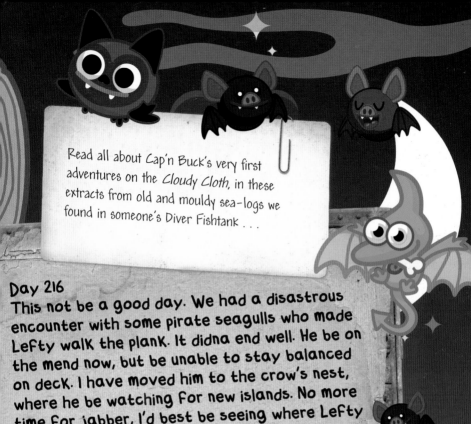

Read all about Cap'n Buck's very first adventures on the *Cloudy Cloth*, in these extracts from old and mouldy sea-logs we found in someone's Diver Fishtank . . .

Day 216

This not be a good day. We had a disastrous encounter with some pirate seagulls who made Lefty walk the plank. It didna end well. He be on the mend now, but be unable to stay balanced on deck. I have moved him to the crow's nest, where he be watching for new islands. No more time for jabber, I'd best be seeing where Lefty thinks we should be goin' next.

Day 359

We be haunting down the scariest treasure ever and have found ourselves on Halloween Island. I be very scared. The sky is as black as Black as Night Wallpaper, and the island looks like a spooky glowing pumpkin. We played a game of eye-spy and spied so many eyes googling at us, they sent shivers up me spine. Then we played lava limbo with the skeleton army. Being a Barnacle, I be very double-jointed so won easily. With my prize we have so much booty to take back to Monstro City, should we make it outta here alive, that is . . . !

39

Day 493

You would'na' believe who we did meet today ... Whilst we be traversin' the deepest, darkest ocean, Lefty spied a strange sight from the crow's nest. It be like a giant Fishy Fountain, and 'twas following us! I climbed to th' top of the mast and used the telescope to see what trouble was in store for us. I soon realized that the something looked very familiar – It was Gail Whale!

"I thought it was you!" Gail shouted, as loud as a cruise ship. "Glad to see you're still adventuring, Bucky!"

"Ahoy there, Gail!" I cheered and explained I were now Cap'n Buck.

I thanked Gail for getting me to Monstro City all that time ago. Without her, I'd never be sailing on the *Cloudy Cloth Clipper* right now! Funny how things turn out, ain't it?!

Around Day 500? I think

We've been lost in time for a whale of a while, bedazzled by Futuristic Falls. We picked up lots of future-fantastic booty goodies, but it's all getting a bit confusing – am I in the past now, and heading to the future, or in the present and heading back into the past? It be all too much. I canna decide whether I is comin or going these days!

Day 637
There's been a few sightings of a dark shadowy figure in an underwater vehicle of late. We've been trying to guess who or what it might be – Billy Bob Baitman gone rogue with a new hat, or Tiddles sporting the latest in Potion Ocean couture? But the hat just didn't seem to fit, so we have come to the thinkin' that it must've been Dr. Strangeglove in a submarine, but we not be certain . . .

Day 640
Gulp! Suspicions were right, the shadow be Dr. Strangeglove and he's been following us for days. We been sailing as fast as we can, but he is always there, hot on our tails. Not sure how I is gonna lose him. Thinking caps on, crew.

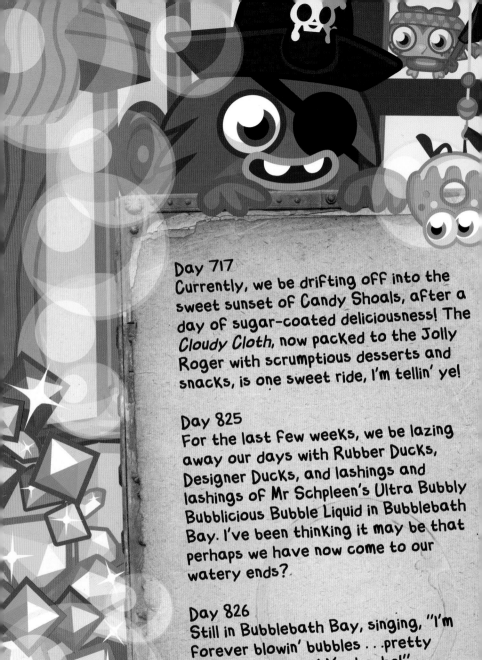

Day 717
Currently, we be drifting off into the sweet sunset of Candy Shoals, after a day of sugar-coated deliciousness! The *Cloudy Cloth*, now packed to the Jolly Roger with scrumptious desserts and snacks, is one sweet ride, I'm tellin' ye!

Day 825
For the last few weeks, we be lazing away our days with Rubber Ducks, Designer Ducks, and lashings and lashings of Mr Schpleen's Ultra Bubbly Bubblicious Bubble Liquid in Bubblebath Bay. I've been thinking it may be that perhaps we have now come to our watery ends?

Day 826
Still in Bubblebath Bay, singing, "I'm forever blowin' bubbles . . . pretty bubbles in the air! Yo, ho, ho!"

Day 827
BB all the way!

Day 828
Yep, still here!

NOTE: We have no record of Buck's days at sea between day 829 and 1999, but I am sure he will no doubt tell us more at a later date.

Day 829
Entire crew turned to prunes, after soaking in BB for too long. Emergency change of plans. Abort mission at Bubblebath Bay and head on to drier pastures. But where I hear ye ask?

Day 1999
I been think'n it bees abou' time for us all aboard the *Cloudy Cloth* to head back to Monstro City. We're all sea dog tired, and we could be doin' with a break from all this adventuring. I ordered th' crew to change course this mornin' and head to the bright lights of the city, so that is what we is doin'. By me calculations we'd should be thar in aboot three days . . .

*** 3 years later ***
(Buck underestimated
the time his journey would
take, just a little.)

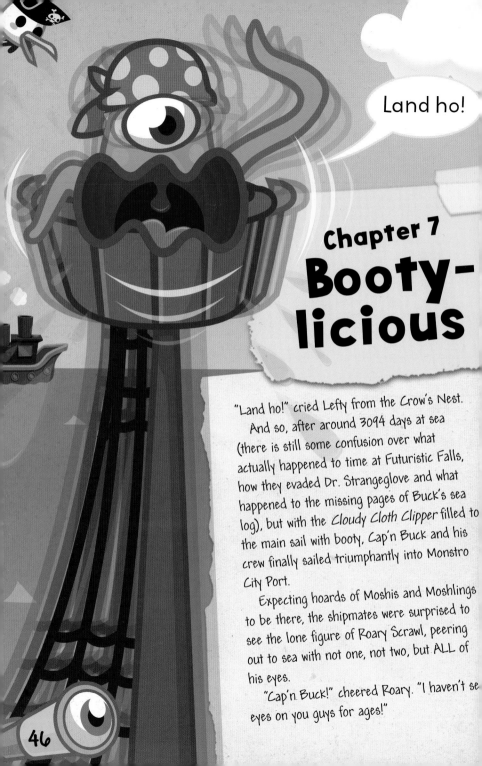

Land ho!

Chapter 7
Booty-licious

"Land ho!" cried Lefty from the Crow's Nest.

And so, after around 3094 days at sea (there is still some confusion over what actually happened to time at Futuristic Falls, how they evaded Dr. Strangeglove and what happened to the missing pages of Buck's sea log), but with the *Cloudy Cloth Clipper* filled to the main sail with booty, Cap'n Buck and his crew finally sailed triumphantly into Monstro City Port.

Expecting hoards of Moshis and Moshlings to be there, the shipmates were surprised to see the lone figure of Roary Scrawl, peering out to sea with not one, not two, but ALL of his eyes.

"Cap'n Buck!" cheered Roary. "I haven't se eyes on you guys for ages!"

"Shiver me timbers!" gasped Buck. "If it ain't me olde friend, Roary."

"Where have you been Cap'n?" asked Roary.

"Arrr! I have traversed afar, dear Roary," said Buck. "And I have many a tall ship tale to tell."

"Eye sea," replied Roary. "And what treasure do you bring the citizens of Monstro City?"

"I be bringin' ye much treasure. The whole *Cloudy Cloth* is full! I canna wait to show it all to you."

"Fantastic!" smiled Roary. "I can't wait to see it!"

"Where are all the land lubbers?" asked Buck.

"We weren't quite sure when to be expecting you, Cap'n," cried Roary. "We did all keep coming down here for 2000 days straight, but after that we gave up a little, I'm afraid. We just didn't know if you'd ever be coming back from your adventures at sea."

"I understand, Roary," said Buck. "We have been adventuring for quite some time. I canna blame youse, but do let everyone know we is here now, with bucketfuls of booty!"

"Don't you worry, I will spread the word. That's what I'm all about. Do you have time for a quick interview for *The Daily Growl?*"

"Aye," replied Buck. "But I be needin' to sort out all this here booty first, so can it wait until later?"

"Of course," nodded Roary. "See you later, shipmater!"

Cap'n Buck, Lefty and all their shipmates anchored down and docked into The Port, where they set up their booty shop. Word soon got around that they had arrived (thanks to Roary putting a massive article in *The Daily Growl*), and queues of Moshis and Moshlings formed from the *Cloudy Cloth* all across The Port. Everyone was eager to get a bite of the booty!

"What a success our time at sea has been," said Buck to Lefty later that day. "We be doing a rrroaring trade today!"

"Speaking of rrroaring, isn't it abou' time you go an' see Roary?" asked Lefty.

" 'tis indeed, my friend. I'll be back in a jiffy."

So, Buck went off to meet Roary and told him a few shark snipbits of his adventures at sea and about some of the collections of booty he found.

"Wow!" gasped Roary. "You have been busy!"

"Arrr!" smiled Buck. "And it has always been my dream to have a life on the sea, with my own crew – and it came true!"

But Buck wanted to keep some of his pioneering secret and certainly did not want to upset others with what he knew to be utterly dangerous adventures, so he only gave a few hints as to some of the sights and battles he experienced.

"Potion Ocean be a very treacherous and unpredictable place yer see, Roary," said Buck. " 'tis best I keep some things to meself."

"But you don't want to keep your treasures to yourself?!" joked Roary.

"Yo, ho, ho!" laughed Buck. "No, no, no! Me treasures will all be shared in my new shop on-board the *Cloudy Cloth*. You should head on down there when you get a chance, Roary."

"I'm SO there," replied Roary. "I've just been waiting for the queues to 'dive' down a little!"

"So, can ye tell me, what's been happenin' in Monstro City?" asks Buck.

"You've been away for about 3094 days now, so . . ." (Roary thought for a while.) "So, quite a lot really Buck! How long have you got?"

"Well, I've been thinking, that me and me shipmates should probably be heading off soon to collect more booty."

"Sounds like a plan, Cap'n, but why are you off so soon?"

"The sea is where I belong, Roary, and it's what I knows best. I canna be stayin' on land too long with these here shaky sea legs!"

"Well, just promise us, you'll keep coming back to share your stories and your booty with us Cap'n!"

"Of course I will!" said Buck. "Until next time, Roary!"

"Until next time, Buck, and happy sailing!"

So, Buck sold the rest of his booty to the hoards of eager Moshis. On doing so, he met more residents of Monstro City than ever before . . .

Obsessed with getting his paws on anything he can make something with, Dewy came by to see what he could buy. Dewy is a real DIY kind of guy.

Looking for items of the highest standard, Mizz Snoots, who usually only hung out at Horrods, came on-board for a snoot around.

Raarghly came in for a spot of out-of-this-world booty.

Even Bushy Fandango came on-board for a nose around her competition.

Agony Ant came to buy a few bits, but also to tell Buck his fortune.

"Your shop will be very successful, Cap'n Buck," she began, "But you will feel the draw of the sea very soon."

"You be right there, Agony Ant!" replied Buck.

Buck made time to stop by at a FizzBangs gig.

Buck also met Gilbert Finnster, shop owner and lover of Moshlings; Monstro City's Ice Scream Man, Giuseppe Gelato; Max Volume with his mega-amped boom box; Weevil Kneevil, Main Street's only courier and lots of celebrities including Broccoli Spears, looking for hair extensions, the Goo Fighters in search of anything with goo in it, and even Taylor Miffed!

Very soon, the entire load of booty was all gone and Buck had met pretty much all the monsters in Monstro City!

"Phew! What a busy day, but I is lovin' sellin' all our booty!" Buck gasped. "But now it must be time to get back on the water."

So, the captain prepared the *Cloudy Cloth*, gathered all his shipmates together, and they headed out into Potion Ocean for more booty-ful adventures . . .

54

Chapter 8
Sea Legend
Lives on

. . . And that has been what they've been doing ever since! (Although Buck's adventures are much shorter than 3094 days long these days.)

Present Day Buck

To this day, Buck has still not been to enough islands, collected enough booty, or partaken of enough adventure to satisfy his needs. He continues to search the seas on the *Cloudy Cloth* with his trusty shipmates and return to Monstro City with treasure. Bringing Twistmas gifts, Fangsgiving Food, Halloween sweets and treats, and many, many more pieces of eight and bags of booty. He's always very welcome at The Port!

Many believe that Buck will probably never go back to his life of grime and grabbing in the shady shallows, but I know that he hopes he'll be reunited with his ma and pa and some of his sea-normous family of Barnacles one day. (As long as they don't call him 'Hairy-Bucky', that is.) You'd think that with 8002 Barnacles out there, another one would be bound to pop up in Monstro City sooner or later!

Buck hopes to continue to live out all of his dreams from when he was lost out at sea after the terrible storm that separated him from his family. It looks to me like he seems to be doing a pretty good job so far! Roary Scrawl reports that Buck 'has never been happier' and is 'leading the life of Raleigh – Sir Walter, to be more precise!'

The Daily Growl

Buck to the future!

Agony Ant has predicted that Buck and the crew of the *Cloudy Cloth Clipper's* future is sure to be plentiful with him at the helm. And she's always right, so that must be true!

The end?

So that concludes Cap'n Buck's Monstrous Biography, 'me hearties', and for now it is time to say – THE END. But you and I both know that Buck, Lefty and the *Cloudy Cloth's* Potion Ocean adventures will never end, not for a whale of a while at least! By now, you should know almost all there is to know about Cap'n Buck's past, present and future. To keep up with all his adventures, you can keep an eye out in *The Daily Growl*. Roary Scrawl is Cap'n Buck's first port of call at The Port, so you can learn of all Buck's latest pioneering pirating days in the interviews he gives for the paper!

Booty Catalogue

Check out this super glooper catalogue of pirate booty that Buck uses to order up all his awesome accessories to keep the *Cloudy Cloth Clipper* looking shipshape! Sorry folks, only monsters who are sailing the Seventy Seas can get hold of most of this booty, but keep an eye out in Monstro City's shops for pirate items like the Cuddly Pirate, Aarrr! Pirate Flag and the Buccaneer's Eyepatch to deck your monster out in seafaring style!

Diving Suit

For when you're feeling deep
One scareful owner

Troubled by Scurvy?

Lefty Lemonade is for you! Rich in vitamins and iron, it'll keep your howl going long after midnight.

BABS' BOUTIQUE

Something fishy? We have it!
Call down to sea us at The Port

Old Ship's Log

Genuine Antique Ship's Log

Will only go up in value

Submarine

Get to the bottom of it!

10 YEAR LEAKING GUARANTEE

Special Offal

Like Dust?

The dust fluster will create more dust than any other leading brand or your money back.

Snapper

Record your adventures on the Potion Ocean with this Snapper.

Get Scrawling

Fancy writing your own biography? You'll need this then. Runs on Growl OSX Comes with a free candle

Rox Box

Keep them safe with this impregnable sea chest.

Fitted with a five lever dreadlock

Round Table

Suitable for the frights of the round table

* Frights not included, or chairs

Croakconut Juice

Sold in a handy spill proof container

* Hammer needed to open.

BIZARRE BAZAAR

Cuddly Pirates now on sale, only 50 Rox!

Dodgy Dealz

Fed up being a pirate? Need to offload that eyepatch? Got too much treasure? Come and see us!

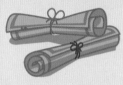

Treasure Maps

It could be you!

Lights

Illuminate something

Roaring Boat

Truely Roarsome

Sea Squash

Lots of stuff squashed into a delightful drink

Do you feel like you're drifting through life?

Can't stay in one place? You need an anchor!

FREE CHAIN INCLUDED

Skull and Cross Bones

Call yourself a pirate?
Not without one
of these you're not
Get One

House Boat

Can't choose between
a house or boat?
Get Both

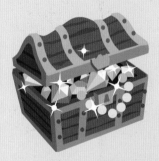

Treasure Chest

Stuffed full of
pirate bounty

* Image may differ
from actual product

Fish-n-mix

A lot of flippy flappy
squidgy stuff to choose from

YUKEA

DECK YOUR SHIP'S DECK OUT IN STYLE